This book is dedicated to
friends! Any time you
need one they are
there for you!
HUGS!

StrauberryStudios Press
a division of strauberry studios

Thunder and Lightning Isn't So Frightening!
Written and illustrated by Susan Straub-Martin

For information regarding permission, please write to:
Permissions Department,
StrauberryStudios Press
11000 NE 10th St. #230
Bellevue, WA 98004

Thunder and Lightning Isn't So Frightening!

Summary: It had been raining hard all day in Brambleberry Hollow, but it was about to get much worse. The thunder boomed and the lightning crashed, Archie and Henri were scared of all of it. See how they overcame their fears and earned their Adventure Scout Badges for bravery.

ISBN# 978-0-9830321-4-4

(1. Fiction 2.Picture Book 3.Humorous Story)
Printed in the USA.

Illustrated using a variety of tools, Camera, Illustrator, photoshop, painter.

Snow Cone Flavors
Lemon • Peach
Blueberry • Boysenberry
Brambleberry • Orange
Strawberry • Salmon
Blackberry • Catfish
Mullberry • Shrimp

SNOW CONES

It had been raining all day in Brambleberry Hollow.
It was cold, wet and just plain soggy. The Snow Cone Palace
had been slow all day.
Poppy and Archie went upstairs to bake cookies.

"Let's make some lemon tea cookies. That will warm
us up." Poppy said in a cheery voice.
Archie loves lemon cookies, Archie loves all kinds of cookies.

"We should make enough to take over
to our friends, the bears, maybe Theo can whip up some tea
and honey to go with them."

"We are all packed up Archie, let's go see if Lemon
wants to go with us to see the bears
and take them some cookies!"

"Do you want to go with us Lemon?" Asked Poppy.

"There hasn't been a customer in all day. Let me close up The Snow Cone Palace and grab the umbrella." said Lemon

They were on their way to visit with the bears,
when all of the sudden a bright flash of lightning,
followed by...
"KABOOM, CRASH, RUMBLE!!!!"
Archie let out a great big "WOOF!"

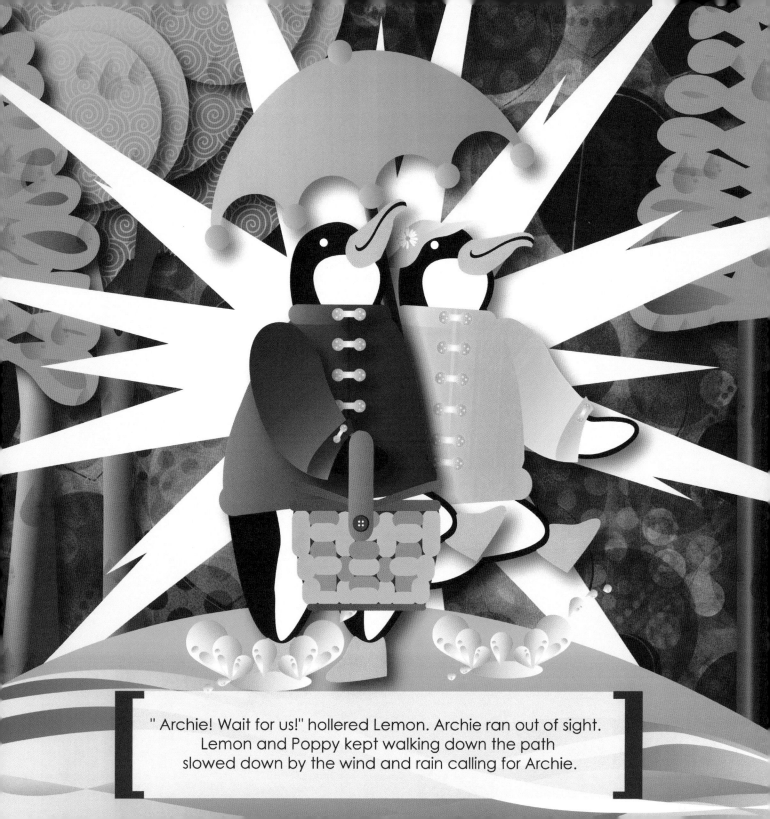

" Archie! Wait for us!" hollered Lemon. Archie ran out of sight.
Lemon and Poppy kept walking down the path
slowed down by the wind and rain calling for Archie.

"Archie, Archie where are you?
I hope he is OK, he was really scared.
I didn't know he was so afraid of thunder
and lightning." Poppy said sadly.

" Hey guys have you seen Archie? We were on our way to see you and he was scared off by the thunderstorm." Said Poppy in a concerned voice.

"Archie and Henri are a pair of scaredy cats, they are in the tent in Henri's room." said Frosty shaking his head. "You have cookies! Theo make some tea, Poppy and Lemon brought fresh baked cookies."

"Hot tea is ready so come on out from hiding, Poppy and Lemon are here with fresh baked cookies. Let's stay indoors by the fireplace and visit." said Theo

"No way it's still storming out! " said Henri.

"You are safe inside with all of us, nothing will happen." Theo insisted.

"There is nothing to be afraid of guys. Think of the thunder like those big timpani drums from the Opera. You know, they are really deep and go **boom, boom, boom**, just like the thunder."
Theo said trying to calm down his friends.

"What about the lightning, it's really scary too." Said Henri.

Theo thought for a minute, "The lightning is like the cymbals, they reflect the lights when they are hit together sending light flashes around the theater."

"That is a good way to look at it, I had never thought of that before. It's OK Archie, we can stay in and eat cookies until the storm stops." said Henri

Archie and Henri joined their friends and ate
cookies and talked the rest of the afternoon.
"These are really good cookies Poppy.
You and Archie had a great idea." Said Lemon

"Thank you for bringing them by. It is nice to have friends visit. It makes a soggy day sunny." Said Frosty

"To Henri and Archie, the Thunder and Lightning badge, for courage in a storm."
Said Frosty Head Adventure Scout.

The End

Lemon Tea Cookies

1/2 cup butter or margarine
3/4 c. sugar
1 Tbs. freshly grated lemon peel
1 tsp. baking powder
1/4 tsp. baking soda
1 egg
1/3 c. milk
2 tsp. lemon juice
1 3/4 c. all-purpose flour
1/4 c. sugar
2 Tbs. Freshly Squeezed lemon juice

In a large mixing bowl beat the butter or margarine with an electric mixer on med. to high speed for 30 seconds. Add the 3/4 cup of sugar, lemon peel, baking powder, and baking soda. Beat til combined, scraping sides of bowl occasionally. Beat in egg, milk, and 2 tsp. lemon juice till combined. Beat in as much of the flour as you can with the mixer. Stir in reamining flour.

Drop dough by rounded teasponss 2 inches apart on an ungreased cookie sheet. Bake in a 350 degree oven for 10 to 12 minutes or till edges are lightly browned. Transfer cookies to wire rack and let cool.

Stir together 1/4 c. sugar and 2 Tbs. lemon juice; brush on cookies when hot.

Makes about 48 cookies.

Written and illustrated by Susan Straub-Martin
Visit: StrauberryStudios.com
for information about the purchase of Buddies.

HOMESAFETY

Acknowledgements

With special thanks to the following:
My family – my husband, Stan Goldstein,
daughter, Sharon Casertano, and sons, Steve,
David and Larry and my mother,
Gertrude Leeds, for their support and
encouragement.
I also want to thank Susan Chidakel, my editor.

I want to dedicate this book to my two young grandsons, Nicholas and Matthew. They were my inspiration in writing this book.